"Where has the water gone?" Simba wondered.

The three friends set off to solve the mystery. They followed the dusty riverbed looking for the water.

As they rounded a bend and peered through the jungle foliage they saw what was wrong. A huge tree had fallen across the river and blocked it.

Simba, Pumbaa and Timon had spent most of the morning relaxing in the jungle. It was always one of their favorite pastimes, but the three friends were getting a bit bored.

"What do you want to do now?" Simba asked with a yawn.

Timon had a great idea! "Let's go to the waterfall for a swim!" he suggested. Everyone agreed that it would be fun.

But when the friends reached the waterfall, they got a terrible surprise! There was no water falling—just the dried-up riverbed and a few shallow pools.

The river had to be cleared, or their waterfall would be gone. Timon tried in vain to chew through the huge log...

Pumbaa pushed with all his strength...

Simba pulled...but it was no good. The vast tree was just too heavy for them.

"It's no use," said Simba. "We're just not strong enough, but I know who is." With that, Simba leaped away through the jungle to find help.

A little while later he returned with
his old friends Jelani the elephant,
and Zazu, the bossy hornbill.
First the mighty Jelani tried to push
the tree with his long tusks.

Before he flew away, Zazu shouted orders to everyone telling them to gather strong vines to tie around the tree and themselves.

On the riverbank, Simba and Pumbaa helped
Jelani pull. Timon saved his strength to shout
instructions and encouragement from the
dry riverbed. Pumbaa tried to warn his
friend that he should stand somewhere else.

"Just pull, Pumbaa," Timon answered.
"I'll give the orders here!"

Suddenly the tree moved and the river rushed toward Timon.

"AAAAARGH!"

He cried as the water washed him downstream.

Luckily help was near! Simba's huge paw gently
snatched Timon from the swirling water.

At last, everything was back to normal at the
waterfall—well, almost everything. Simba and
Pumbaa splashed in the river. But little Timon
was happy just to watch from the bank. He'd
had quite enough water for one day!